LITTLE LIL AND THE SWING-SINGING SAX

LITTLE LIL AND THE SWING-SINGING SAX

by LIBBA MOORE GRAY

Illustrated by LISA COHEN

Simon & Schuster Books for Young Readers

*Special thanks to Nat and John at National Art and Hobby
in New Orleans for their supplies and support.*

— L. C.

SIMON & SCHUSTER BOOKS FOR YOUNG READERS
An imprint of Simon & Schuster Children's Publishing Division
1230 Avenue of the Americas, New York, New York 10020
Text copyright © 1996 by the Estate of Libba Moore Gray
Illustrations copyright © 1996 by Lisa Cohen
SIMON & SCHUSTER BOOKS FOR YOUNG READERS is a trademark of
Simon & Schuster.
Book design by Lucille Chomowicz
The text for this book is set in Weidemann
The illustrations are rendered in acrylic on paper
Printed and bound in Hong Kong by the South China Printing
Co. (1988) Ltd. First Edition
10 9 8 7 6 5 4 3 2 1
Library of Congress Cataloging-in-Publication Data
Gray, Libba Moore.
   Little Lil and the swing-singing sax / by Libba Moore Gray ;
illustrated by Lisa Cohen. — 1st ed.
               p.   cm.
   Summary: When Little Lil's mother gets sick, Uncle Sudi Man
pawns his saxaphone to buy medicine, but Little Lil knows that
it is her uncle's jazz music that will really help her mother feel
better.
   ISBN 0-689-80681-7 (alk. paper)
   [1. Family life—Fiction. 2. Music—Fiction. 3. Saxaphone—
Fiction. 4. Afro-Americans—Fiction.] I. Cohen, Lisa, ill.
II. Title. PZ7.G7793Lm 1996 [E]—dc20 95-362

This book is for Janet Dawson.

—L. M. G.

To my daughter, Mischa and my husband, Sebastien.

—L. C.

Sometimes when the neon lights are blink blink
blinking on the rain-wet streets and the gray steam
climbs the window of the doughnut shop and the
smell of pizzas and pretzels and burgers drift through the air . . . I
remember walking along the big city streets holding the hand of
my fat-cheeked, curly-haired, horn-blowing uncle. His friends called
him Sudi the Music-Making Man, but I called him Uncle Sudi Man,
and have done so all my life.

By day, he ran a big yellow steam shovel that dug up city streets. At night, he blew into a low-moaning saxophone in a swing-singing jazz club where he could make the people laugh and he could make the people cry when he played that sad-sighing horn.

Uncle Sudi Man lived with me and my mama, his sister, and everybody called her Big Lil and they called me Little Lil and we didn't have much money but we had a lot of love and we laughed more than we cried.

One magic night when the moon was hanging low, I begged to go with Uncle Sudi Man but Mama Big Lil said in her mama-loud voice, "Not tonight, child. No. No. No." And then I said, "Mama Big Lil why don't you go, too?" And she threw back her head and laughed out a big, "Why not?"

It was on that night that Mama Big Lil danced lighter than a feather across the cracked linoleum floor, opened the dark closet door, and reached high on the shelf for an old tin box. In that box, wrapped in a scrap of white lace, was a little gold ring with a shining blue stone. It had been my grandmother's ring and Mama Big Lil's ring and now it was to be my ring. I smiled so big I thought my smile would ride off my face when Mama Big Lil took that ring from the box and handed it to me.

And so with Uncle Sudi Man dressed in his fine new duds and smelling of bay rum and Mama Big Lil dressed in her Sunday best dress and smelling of sweet talcum, they took me red ribboned and patent leathered between them to hear my Uncle Sudi Man make the sax sing. And all the time we were walking down that street that ring was shimmering on my finger like star fire under the neon lights.

And the silverware clicked and the dishes clinked and clattered as the people ate and chattered until my Uncle Sudi Man blew into his silver-keyed horn. It was then a sweet hush fell over everything in that good-time place. Mama Big Lil squeezed my hand that wore the little gold ring and happiness filled my heart as Uncle Sudi Man's velvet notes filled the air.

And just when things seemed sweetest, the bad times came. Mama Big Lil took sick . . . too sick to do anything but sit in the big easy chair. Uncle Sudi Man walked like he carried a heavy load, bowed his head often, and whispered to himself. Mama Big Lil needed medicine and medicine meant money and the money wasn't there.

So moving slow and moving weary and sighing like a slow-leaking tire, he walked down the steps and down the street into a shelf-piled trading place called Honest Don's Pawn Shop where he traded in that horn for some wrinkled dollar bills.

Autumn came and autumn went and hallelujah-amen the medicine helped a bit. Mama Big Lil got a little better but the laughter stayed away while the horn gathered dust on a dingy cluttered shelf.

Mama Big Lil's eyes looked far away and when she closed them I knew she heard the lost sounds of Uncle Sudi Man's sax playing in her head and making her heart sad. It was then I knew I had to come up with a plan.

One snowy day in the middle of December I started drawing a picture. And in the picture I drew a tree and under the tree I drew a box and in the box I drew a horn and I drew Uncle Sudi Man and Mama Big Lil and Little Lil . . . me . . . with our heads thrown back all dancing around the tree.

When I finished I ran down the steps and skipped down the street and into the bell-ringing door of the trading place where I offered to trade my art for Uncle Sudi Man's horn. Honest Don looked at it hard but he didn't take the silent sax off the cluttered shelf.

Then I saw Honest Don's eyes go to my sparkling ring. I looked away. I stared at the calendar on the wall. I stared at the light over my head and finally I stared at the sax on the shelf. I swallowed hard to hold back the tears and slowly handed over my beautiful ring with the star-fire stone.

With a gold-toothed smile and a warm "Bless your heart," Honest Don took my Uncle Sudi Man's horn right off the shelf and handed it to me. And oh, I took it gently and cradled it softly like a newborn child. Then Honest Don winked and handed back my blue-stoned ring and hung my picture in the storefront window for all to see. And everyone who saw it smiled and smiled.

When I walked in the door with Uncle Sudi Man's sax Mama Big Lil clapped her hands, stamped her feet, and got out of her chair. Before he came home we found a box and in the box we put the horn and around the box we tied a bright red bow and placed it under the tinseled Christmas tree.

On Christmas morning we danced around the tree
just like in my picture and then Uncle Sudi Man
warmed up that horn with a few wobbly notes.
And soon we were dancing out the door,
up the stairs, and onto the tar roof in
our own special Christmas parade.

So on a snow-swirling day with the neon lights far below us blink blink blinking like an upside-down, cold electric sky, Mama Big Lil and I danced on that flat, black rooftop. Uncle Sudi Man danced, too, his angel-sweet, blue-curling notes rising like a prayer above the white December clouds.